D0555984

The Scarlet Stockings Spy

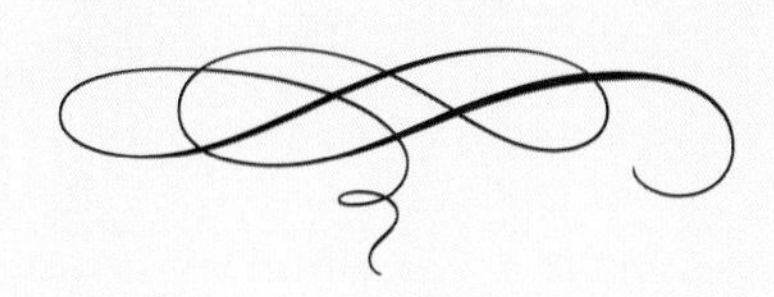

TRINKA HAKES NOBLE ~ *Illustrated by* ROBERT PAPP

For the Maumee Street Writers' Club–
With my deep appreciation.

–THN

It is a wonderful gift to create art. Thank you to
all who have allowed me to share it.

–RP

Sleeping Bear Press
310 North Main Street, Suite 300
Chelsea, MI 48118
www.sleepingbearpress.com

THOMSON
GALE

Printed and bound in Canada.

10 9 8 7 6 5 4 3 2

Library of Congress Cataloging-in-Publication Data
Noble, Trinka Hakes.
The scarlet stockings spy / written by Trinka Hakes Noble ; illustrated by Robert Papp.
p. cm.
Summary: In 1777 Philadelphia, young Maddy Rose spies for General Washington's army by using an unusual code to communicate with her soldier brother.
ISBN 1-58536-230-1
1. Philadelphia (Pa.)–History–1775-1783–Juvenile fiction. [1. Philadelphia (Pa.)–History–1775-1783–Fiction. 2. Spies–Fiction. 3. Brothers and sisters–Fiction. 4. United States–History–Revolution, 1775-1783–Fiction.] I. Papp, Robert, ill. II. Title.
PZ7.N6715Sc 2004
[Fic]–dc22
2004007878

Author's Note

The Scarlet Stockings Spy has deep personal meaning for me because my direct ancestor, James Hakes, was a soldier in the Revolutionary War. He traveled with his Connecticut regiment to Pennsylvania and New Jersey to join Washington's army from September 1776 to March 1777, where they distinguished themselves at the Battles of Trenton and Princeton. I set this story in the same time period.

My ancestor continued to serve in the Continental Army, and in 1780, General Washington visited the Hakes home in Rensselaer, New York, where they were expecting a child. If a boy, the general requested the child be named in his honor. In August of 1780 George Washington Hakes was born and became my great-great-great grandfather.

American history has always been alive for me. Through my writing and storytelling, I am able to transport myself back to the times of my ancestors. In preparation for writing this story, I walked the battlefield at Princeton, New Jersey, retracing the footsteps of my ancestor who fought there 227 years ago. I was deeply moved and felt not only immense gratitude and pride, but a strong connection to those who came before me, to the characters in my story, to my own cherished freedom, and to my own country.

I consider it an honor to have written *The Scarlet Stockings Spy.*

Trinka Hakes Noble

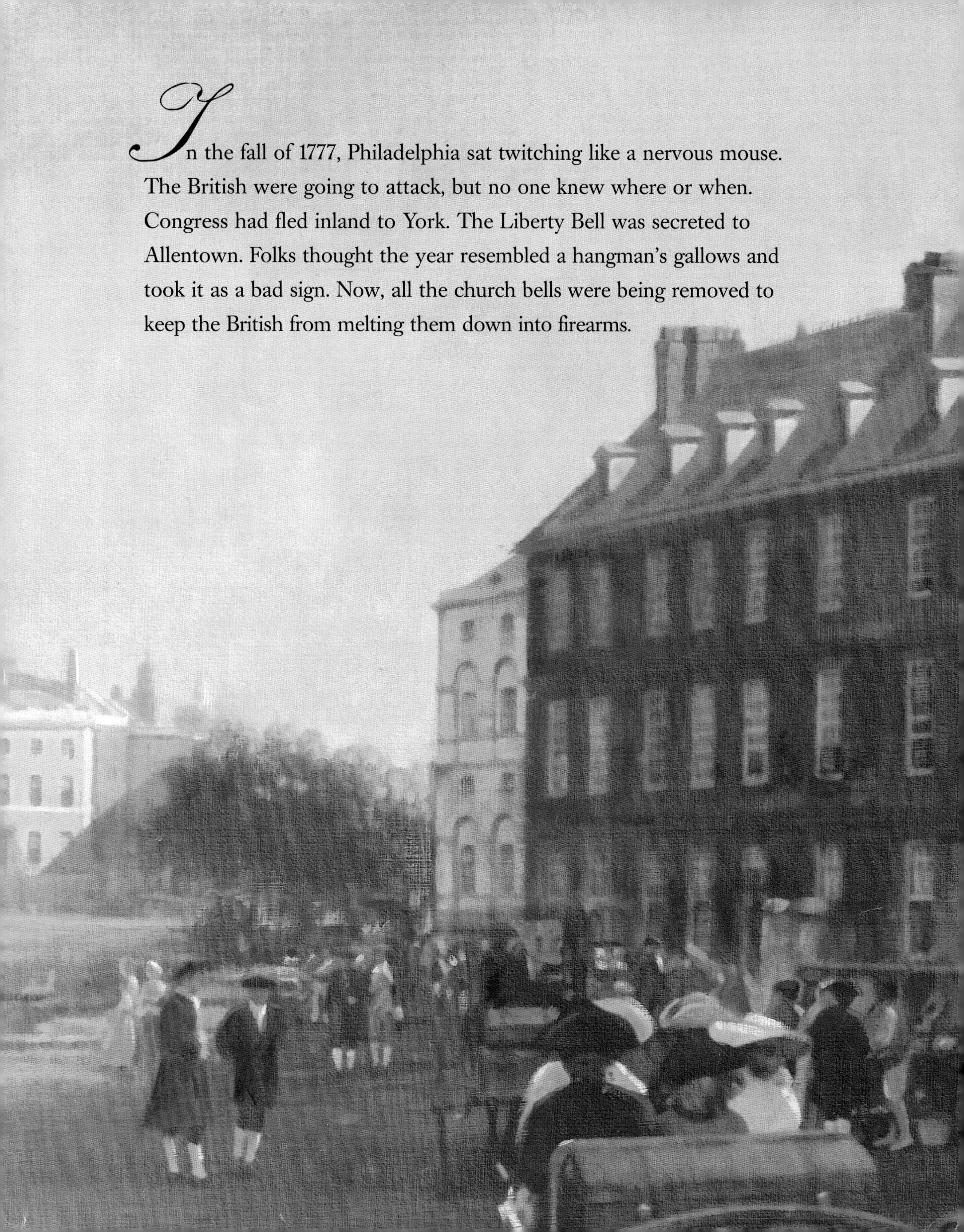

In the fall of 1777, Philadelphia sat twitching like a nervous mouse. The British were going to attack, but no one knew where or when. Congress had fled inland to York. The Liberty Bell was secreted to Allentown. Folks thought the year resembled a hangman's gallows and took it as a bad sign. Now, all the church bells were being removed to keep the British from melting them down into firearms.

Uncertainty settled over the city like soot. Suspicions skulked through the cobblestone streets like hungry alley cats. Rumors multiplied like horseflies. Spies were everywhere.

Some spied for the British, loyal to the king. Others spied for the Patriots, loyal to Washington's army, now camped west of the city. Still other spies were loyal to lining their pockets.

But one little spy moved through the streets unnoticed, even though she wore scarlet stockings. Her name was Maddy Rose and she lived with her mother and brother in the Leather Apron District, next to the harbor, where the city's tradesfolk lived and worked in narrow brick row houses.

“Maddy Rose,” called her mother from the front room, not looking up from her spinning. “Tarry not. Mistress Ross hath need of these linens this morning.”

Dusty eastern light filtered through the panes of thick glass in their tiny row house on Appletree Alley where the *click, clack, click* of the flax wheel never stopped from early dawn ‘til candlelight.

“Yes, Mother,” answered Maddy Rose, hurrying to poke up the fire.

Each morning, before she went to sew seams for Mistress Ross on Arch Street, Maddy Rose lowered the teakettle over the hearth, then crushed dried raspberry leaves to brew Liberty tea. Since the tea rebellion in Boston, drinking imported English tea was considered disloyal.

This morning her mother looked tired, so Maddy Rose added a drop of precious honey. Carefully she carried the only china teacup they owned to her mother, a treasured gift from her father.

“Here, Mother dear. This will refresh you.”

Maddy Rose’s mother stopped spinning and gently held her daughter’s chin.

“You have his strong jaw,” she sighed, her eyes glistening softly.

Maddy Rose knew her mother was remembering her father, who had fallen at the Battle of Princeton last winter and lay with the others beneath the soil of New Jersey. Many men had gone to the war. Even her brother Jonathan, who was only fifteen, had joined Washington’s army to wear the blue coat.

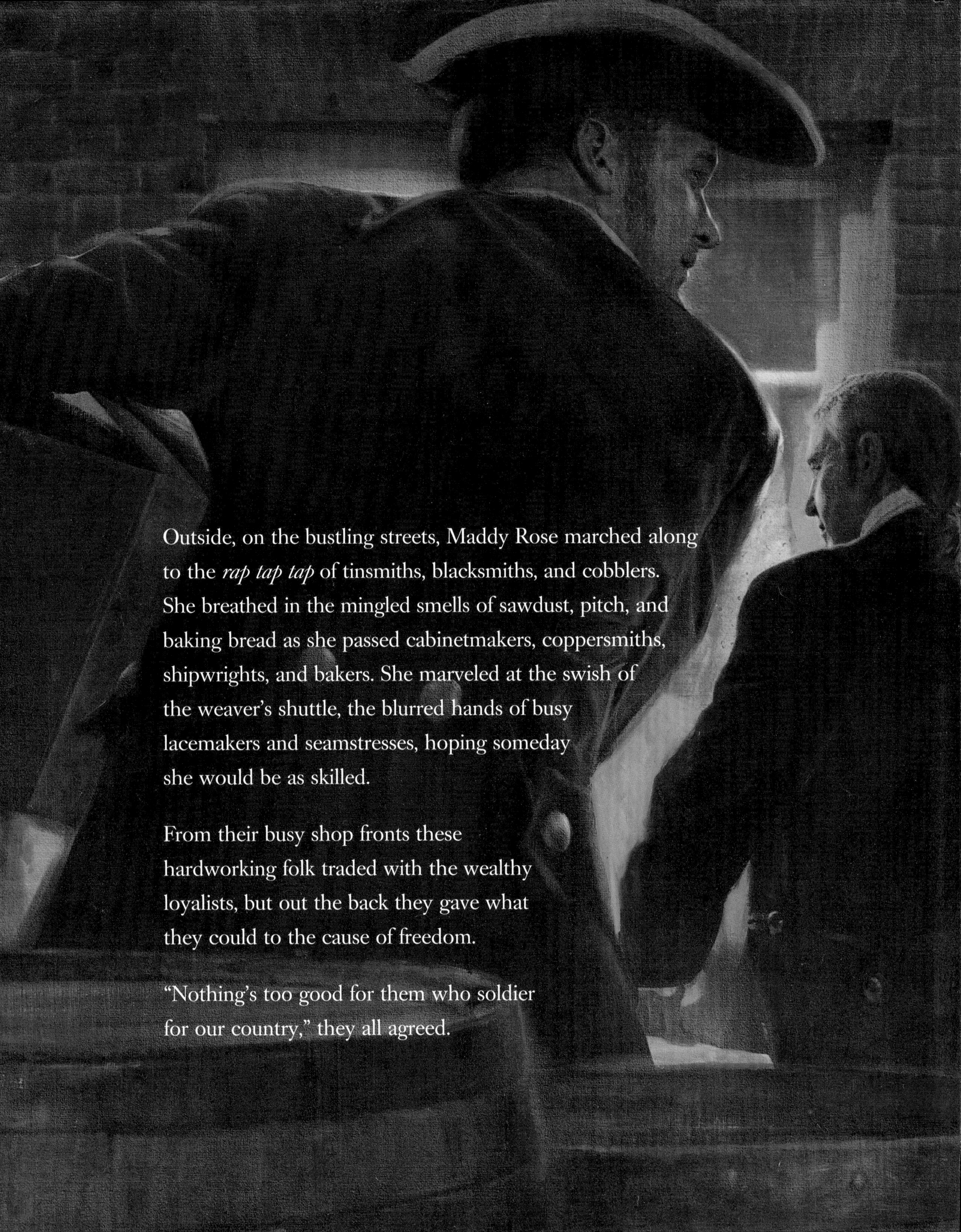

Outside, on the bustling streets, Maddy Rose marched along to the *rap tap tap* of tinsmiths, blacksmiths, and cobblers. She breathed in the mingled smells of sawdust, pitch, and baking bread as she passed cabinetmakers, coppersmiths, shipwrights, and bakers. She marveled at the swish of the weaver's shuttle, the blurred hands of busy lacemakers and seamstresses, hoping someday she would be as skilled.

From their busy shop fronts these hardworking folk traded with the wealthy loyalists, but out the back they gave what they could to the cause of freedom.

"Nothing's too good for them who soldier for our country," they all agreed.

Maddy Rose was loyal only to Jonathan. No one suspected her of anything, of course. Not this hardworking little seamstress who helped her poor mother by earning threepence. Why, she even hung the wash out every week like clockwork. But that's where Maddy Rose fooled them, for it was her small clothesline, hanging from her third-floor window that held a secret code.

She'd lined her clothesline up perfectly with the harbor, just like when she and Jonathan used to play "Harbormaster." Jonathan pretended to be the harbormaster, cupping his hands like a spyglass, barking out docking and departing orders from an upper window. Maddy Rose scrambled below, playing the harbormaster's assistant, arranging cobblestones, apples, and scraps of wood as though they were real ships. Jonathan always tricked her so there would be a collision, then he'd make loud crashing and exploding sounds 'til they both laughed. It was only a game. But now things were different. The country was at war.

So once a week at dusk, using their secret code, Maddy Rose hung out her stockings and petticoats in the same order as the real ships along the wharf. A petticoat was code for a lightweight friendly vessel from the colonies. A scarlet stocking hanging toe up meant a merchant vessel from the islands or foreign port. When the toe hung down, it meant the vessel was suspicious and needed watching. But when the ship was riding low in the water, it meant only one thing–heavy firearms for the British. That's when Maddy Rose would weight that stocking down with a cobblestone.

Maddy Rose agreed too, for she was a Patriot rebel from head to toe in her homespun petticoats, her linsey-woolsey dress and muslin apron, her hand-me-down shoes and woven straw hat. But it was her hand knit scarlet stockings that she valued the most, for their worth was far greater than just warm dry feet.

Whenever Maddy Rose strutted by the fine young ladies of Philadelphia in their creamy white stockings and dainty slippers, she'd flounce her skirts and jut out her proud strong chin.

"Such poppycock!" she'd cluck to herself. No fancy silks, satins, and brocades imported from London for her. To wear such finery showed loyalty to the king.

Jonathan would sneak into the city after dark wearing a disguise, because if a spy were caught, he could be hanged. He'd read her clothesline then steal away through the darkened city to the countryside, relaying the information back to Washington's headquarters, so the Patriots were aware of who might be gunrunners and smugglers for the British.

One time Jonathan disguised himself as a crippled beggar with a cane, limping badly. Maddy Rose became worried. But then he flipped into a perfect handstand, balancing on the cane like an acrobat. Oh how she laughed and clapped.

Once he saluted her like a puffed up rooster, then did an about-face, tripped on purpose, and fell flat as a flapjack, sending her into gales of laughter.

The last time he dressed as a woman, then hiked up his skirts and danced a wild jig in his long johns.

"Oh, Jonathan, you silly goat," Maddy Rose giggled from behind her window, then pulled in her clothesline and slept with a smile on her face.

Then, early one morn...*Ka-BOOM!*

The battle had started. British and Patriot cannons were blasting each other across Brandywine Creek. The ferocious bombardment was so loud that all of Philadelphia could hear it, even though it was twenty-five miles away. The date was September 11th, 1777.

On that same foggy dawn, Jonathan hid in the mist with the Pennsylvania Line, lying low in the barleycorn fields and reedy banks along Brandywine Creek, clutching his musket as cannonballs screeched overhead, waiting for the command to attack the British redcoats on foot.

"Cannons!" Maddy Rose cried out as she tore downstairs. "Mother, do you not hear it?"

"Aye, child," she answered calmly, trying to spin as usual. "Be brave now. Let's get to thy work."

Maddy Rose tried not to think what those thundering cannons meant. She began pounding raspberry leaves as hard as she could. But the harder she pounded, the louder the cannons roared.

Ka-BOOM, BOOM!

She yanked the teakettle from the crane and spun around with the teacup in her hand. Just then…

KA-BOOM, BOOM…KA-BOOM!!

Maddy Rose jumped…and the precious teacup flew from her hand and smashed into a hundred bits and pieces.

The blazing cannons kept up their deadly attack, back and forth across Brandywine Creek 'til midday. Then came the command to charge, and the air became thick with the crack of muskets, the hiss of lead balls, and the acrid stench of gunpowder smoke.

But Maddy Rose could not hear this part of the battle from where she sat in Ross's Upholstery Shop, ripping out seam after seam, unable to concentrate on the required sixteen stitches per inch.

"Maddy Rose, those seams can wait," said Mistress Ross kindly. She was a mild-mannered Quaker woman whose husband had fallen too. "The *Tidewater*'s just docked from the Carolinas. Run down to the harbor and fetch my order of cotton batting and bindings."

"Yes, Ma'am," answered Maddy Rose eagerly. She needed to survey the harbor, for Jonathan would come soon after dark.

Maddy Rose's sharp eyes swept over the many ships crowded along the wharf. She memorized their positions, and which would be petticoats, which would be stockings with toes up, or toes down, but on this day she was startled to see that many stockings would need cobblestone weights.

Quickly she fetched Mistress Ross's order, but before she left, something made her look across the Delaware toward New Jersey, and her heart nearly stopped! For there, in the middle of the river, hiding among the many moored ships, sat a British man-of-war!

"Jonathan must know this!" she gasped.

Maddy Rose raced back and set to work. It was the heaviest

But that night Jonathan didn't come; yet Maddy Rose kept watch for him long into that black night. He didn't come the next night either, or the next, nor the one after that. More and more nights passed, yet she kept looking for him from her window, never losing hope.

Then, one night, a shadowy figure stood in Jonathan's place. She snuffed out her candle and peeked over the darkened sill. Who was he? Could it be Jonathan? But when he saw her window go dark he turned to leave.

Maddy Rose didn't even stop to think or slip on her shoes. She bounded after him, darting in and out of the shadows between the lampposts, stalking him like a silent cat in her stocking feet through the damp streets.

"Jonathan?" she whispered hopefully, shyly touching his cloak. "Is that you?"

The stranger turned and smiled. “I’m Seth,” he answered. “And by the looks of your feet, you must be Little Miss Scarlet Stockings, Jonathan’s sister.”

“You know him? You know my brother?” she choked. Her face flushed hot and her throat tightened as she waited for Seth’s answer.

But Seth was silent. Damp night air drifted in from the Delaware River, brushed against Maddy Rose’s burning cheeks and seeped into Seth’s eyes as he stared hard into the darkness. Then, solemnly, he bowed his head and spoke in a low voice.

“I’m proud to say I did, Miss.”

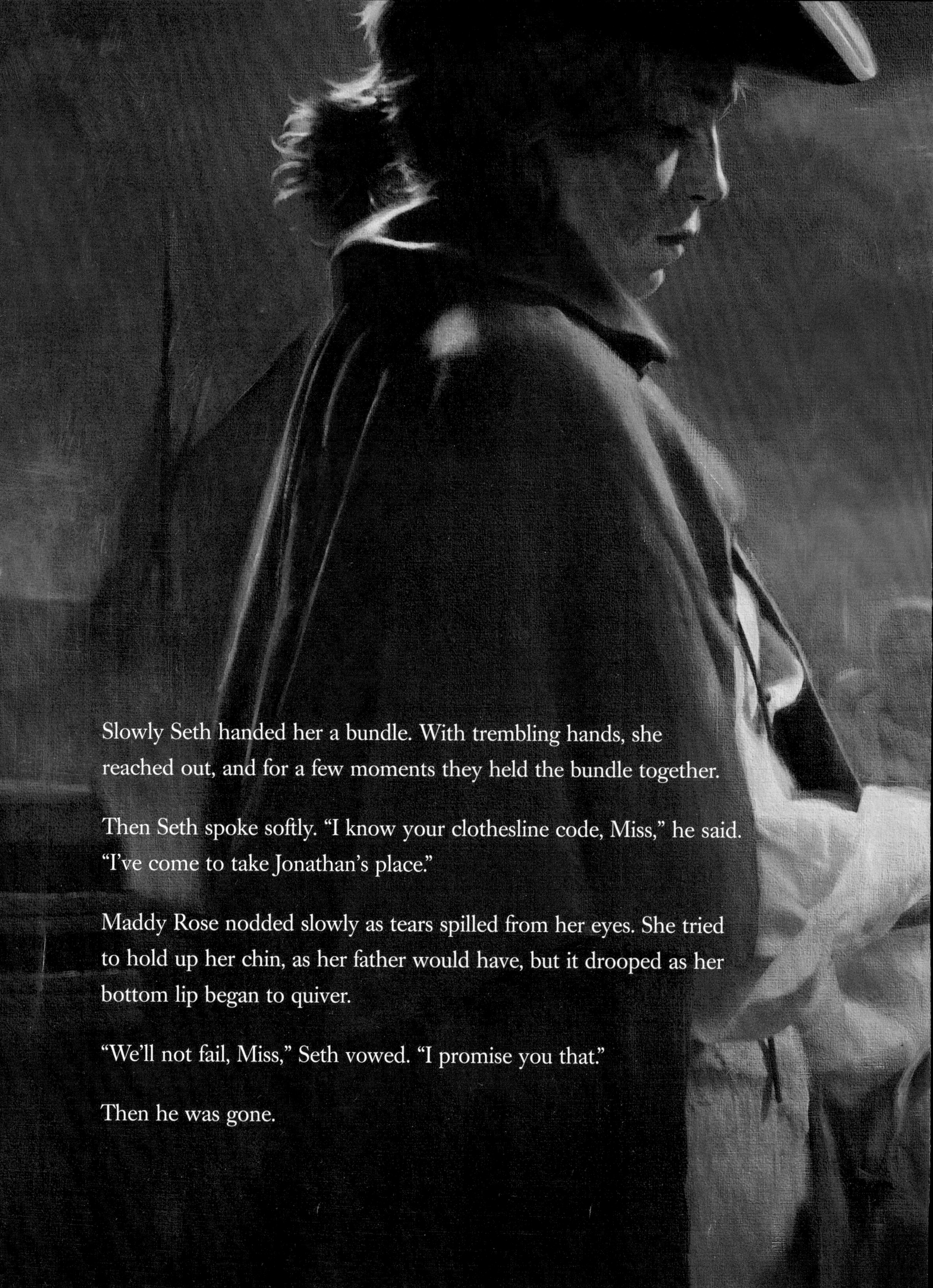

Slowly Seth handed her a bundle. With trembling hands, she reached out, and for a few moments they held the bundle together.

Then Seth spoke softly. "I know your clothesline code, Miss," he said. "I've come to take Jonathan's place."

Maddy Rose nodded slowly as tears spilled from her eyes. She tried to hold up her chin, as her father would have, but it drooped as her bottom lip began to quiver.

"We'll not fail, Miss," Seth vowed. "I promise you that."

Then he was gone.

Back in her darkened room, Maddy Rose slowly untied the bundle. It was Jonathan's blue coat. Tenderly, she let her small fingers explore the blue wool serge until she found it–a stiff dried bloodstain. Then, with her littlest finger, she lightly traced two letters on the pewter buttons–U.S.

"Us," she whispered in the dark, "...for us, dear brother...for all of us."

That night, and for many nights to follow, Maddy Rose sat in her tiny room lit by a single candle, threaded her needle and sewed. She was making an American flag from her scarlet stockings, her white petticoats, and her brother's blue coat. And sewn into every one of her stitches was a tear of grief and the clenched fist of defiance.

Through the bleak cold winter that followed, Washington's army retreated to Valley Forge while the British occupied Philadelphia, lock, stock, and barrel. At night the redcoat invaders celebrated with military balls and fancy cotillions. And during the day they patrolled the streets, eyes forward, never noticing a young girl's unmentionables hanging overhead on a small clothesline from a third-floor window.

In the spring of 1778 the British left Philadelphia, crossed the Delaware, and were sent running by Washington's army at the Battle of Monmouth in New Jersey. The Patriots of Philadelphia celebrated, flying flags everywhere!

But there was one little flag that hung by itself on a small clothesline high over Appletree Alley. And fresh spring breezes traveled from New Jersey and found the little flag and lifted it up high. How proud and strong it flew, just like her father's chin, for it was Maddy Rose's scarlet stockings flag.

Many years have passed since the spring of 1778. No one knows for sure what happened to this little flag. But if by chance you found it, in an old trunk or dusty attic or barn loft or musty museum basement, you would notice that one star is bigger than the rest. It sits in a place of honor, at the top of an arch of thirteen stars in a field of blue, the keystone star for Pennsylvania. And if you looked under that star, you would find a musket ball hole.